D1491125

Fairy Tale Classics

VIKING Published by Penguin Group, Penguin Young Readers Group, 345 Hudson Street, New York, New York 10014, U.S.A. Penguin Books Ltd, 80 Strand, London WC2R 0RL, England. Penguin Books Australia Ltd, 250 Camberwell Road, Camberwell, Victoria 3124, Australia. Penguin Books Canada Ltd, 10 Alcorn Avenue, Toronto, Ontario, Canada M4V 3B2. Penguin Books (N.Z.) Ltd, 182-190 Wairau Road, Auckland 10, New Zealand

Little Red Riding Hood first published in 2000 by Viking, a division of Penguin Putnam Books for Young Readers. *The Gingerbread Boy* first published in 1995 by Viking, a division of Penguin Books USA Inc. *Henny-Penny* first published in 1997 by Viking, a division of Penguin Books USA Inc. *The Princess and the Pea* first published in 1996 by Viking, a division of Penguin Books USA Inc. *The Magic Porridge Pot* first published in 1997 by Viking, a division of Penguin Books USA Inc. *The Little Red Hen* first published in 1995 by Viking, a division of Penguin Books USA Inc. *The Ugly Duckling* first published in 1997 by Viking, a division of Penguin Books USA Inc.

The Fairy Tale Classics Easy-to-Read Collection published in 2003 by Viking, a division of Penguin Young Readers Group.

10 9 8 7 6 5 4 3 2 1

EASY-TO-READ COLLECTION

Fairy Tale Classics

by HARRIET ZIEFERT

illustrated by EMILY BOLAM

VIKING

Contents

Little Red Riding Hood

retold by Harriet Ziefert

illustrated by Emily Bolam

Little Red Riding Hood
lived with her mother
in a little house
near the woods.

One day her mother said,
"Your grandmother is sick.
These cakes will make
her feel better.
Will you take them to her?"

12

"I will," said Little Red
Riding Hood.

"Be careful," said her mother.
"Don't talk to any strangers
on the way."

"I will be careful," said
Little Red Riding Hood.
"I will not talk to strangers."

Little Red Riding Hood
waved to a woodcutter.
Then she met a wolf.

"Good morning,"
said the wolf.
"Where are you going?"

"I'm taking cakes
to my grandmother.
She is sick."

"Why don't you take her
some flowers, too?"
said the wolf.

"What a good idea!" said
Little Red Riding Hood.

Little Red Riding Hood
picked some flowers.
And the wolf ran off to
Grandma's house.

"Who is there?"
asked Grandma.

"It's me—it's
Little Red Riding Hood,"
said the wolf in a high voice.

RAT-TAT
TAT!

"Come in, my dear,"
said Grandma.

The wolf went right to
Grandma's bedroom.

And he had himself
a very good meal.

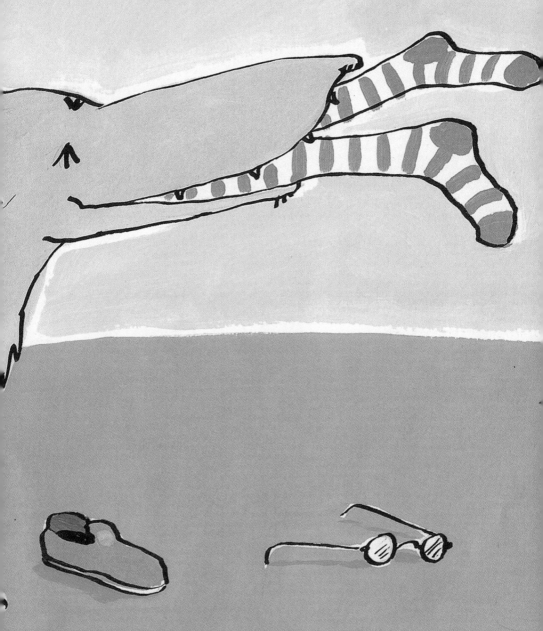

The wolf waited for
Little Red Riding Hood.

Before long, he heard
a knock at the door.

"Come in, my dear,"
said the wolf.

Little Red Riding Hood said,
"Oh, Grandma—what big eyes
you have."

"The better to see you with,
my dear," said the wolf.

"Oh, Grandma—what big ears you have," said Little Red Riding Hood.

"The better to hear you with,
my dear," said the wolf.

"Oh, Grandma—what big teeth you
have," said Little Red Riding Hood.

"The better to EAT you with,
my dear!" said the wolf.

"You're not my grandma,"
said Little Red Riding Hood.
But it was too late.

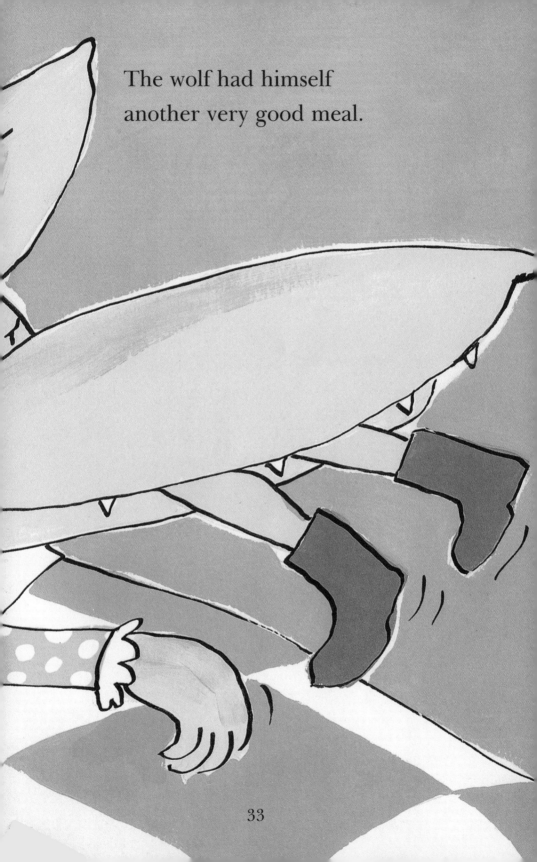

The wolf had himself
another very good meal.

The woodcutter saw the open door
and went inside.

As soon as he saw the wolf,
he lifted his ax and . . .

killed the wolf.

Little Red Riding Hood
and her grandmother
stepped out.

From that day on,
Little Red Riding Hood
never, ever talked to
strangers again.

The Gingerbread Boy

retold by Harriet Ziefert

illustrated by Emily Bolam

A little old man
and a little old woman
lived in a little old house.

They had no children.

The little old woman
wanted a little boy.
So she made a boy
out of gingerbread.

Then she put him
in the oven to bake.

The little old woman
opened the oven door.

Out jumped the little
gingerbread boy and . . .

away he ran—out of
the little old house!
"Stop! Stop!"
said the little old woman.

"Stop! Stop!"
   said the little old man.

But the little gingerbread
boy said:
"Run, run, as fast as you can.
You can't catch me—
I'm the gingerbread man!"

The little gingerbread boy
ran on and on.
He ran past a cow.
"Stop! Stop!"
said the cow.

But the little gingerbread
boy said:
"I have run away
from a little old woman
and a little old man.
I can run away from you—I can!"

The little gingerbread boy
ran on and on.
He ran past a horse.
"Stop! Stop!" said the horse.

But the little gingerbread
boy said:
"I have run away from
a little old woman,
a little old man, and a cow.
I can run away from you—I can!"

The little gingerbread boy
ran on and on.
He ran past a farmer.

"Stop! Stop!"
said the farmer.
But the little gingerbread
boy said:

"I have run away from
a little old woman,
a little old man,
a cow, and a horse.
I can run away from you—I can!"

The little gingerbread boy
ran on and on until
he came to a river.
Then he stopped.

A fox was running by.
He saw the gingerbread boy.
He knew the gingerbread boy
would make a good snack.

The fox was smart.

He said to the gingerbread boy,

"I'll help you cross the river.

Sit on my tail."

The little gingerbread boy
sat on the fox's tail.

The fox began to swim
across the river.

"You're getting wet,"
said the fox.
"Why don't you jump
onto my back?"

The little gingerbread boy
jumped onto the fox's back.

Then the fox said:
"You are too heavy
to sit on my back.
Why don't you jump
onto my head?"

Then the fox said:
"You are still too heavy.
Why don't you jump
onto my nose?"

So the little gingerbread boy
jumped onto the fox's nose.

Then the fox turned
his head and . . .

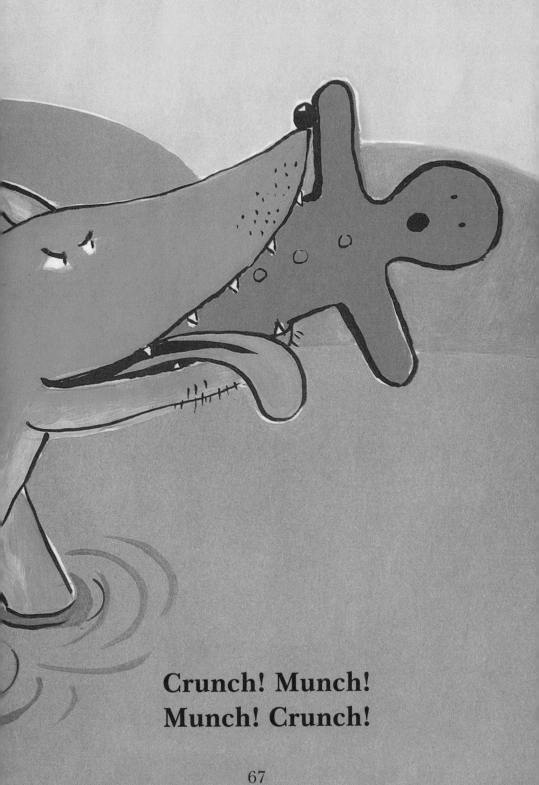

Crunch! Munch!
Munch! Crunch!

The little gingerbread boy
was all gone!

Henny-Penny

retold by Harriet Ziefert

illustrated by Emily Bolam

One day Henny-Penny
went for a walk.
An acorn fell.

The acorn hit Henny-Penny
on the head!

"Oh, dear," said Henny-Penny.
"The sky is falling.
    I must go and tell the king."

On her way she met Cocky-Locky.

"Where are you going?"
asked Cocky-Locky.

"I am going to tell the king
the sky is falling,"
said Henny-Penny.

"I'll come with you,"
said Cocky-Locky.

On the way they met Ducky-Lucky.
"Where are you going?"
asked Ducky-Lucky.

"We are going to tell the king
the sky is falling," they said.

"I'll come with you,"
said Ducky-Lucky.

On the way they met Goosey-Loosey.

"Where are you going?"
asked Goosey-Loosey.

"We are going to tell the king
the sky is falling," they said.

"I'll come with you,"
said Goosey-Loosey.

On the way they met Turkey-Lurkey.
"Where are you going?"
asked Turkey-Lurkey.

"We are going to tell the king
 the sky is falling," they said.
"I'll come with you,"
 said Turkey-Lurkey.

Then they met Foxy-Loxy.
"Where are you going?"
asked Foxy-Loxy.

"We are going to tell the king
the sky is falling," they said.

"You are not going the right way,"
said Foxy-Loxy. "I will show you
a good way to go."

So they followed Foxy-Loxy.

He stopped in front of a dark hole. "This is a good way to go to the king," said Foxy-Loxy.

Foxy-Loxy went in first.
Turkey-Lurkey followed him.

Goosey-Loosey went in next.

Ducky-Lucky followed Goosey-Loosey.

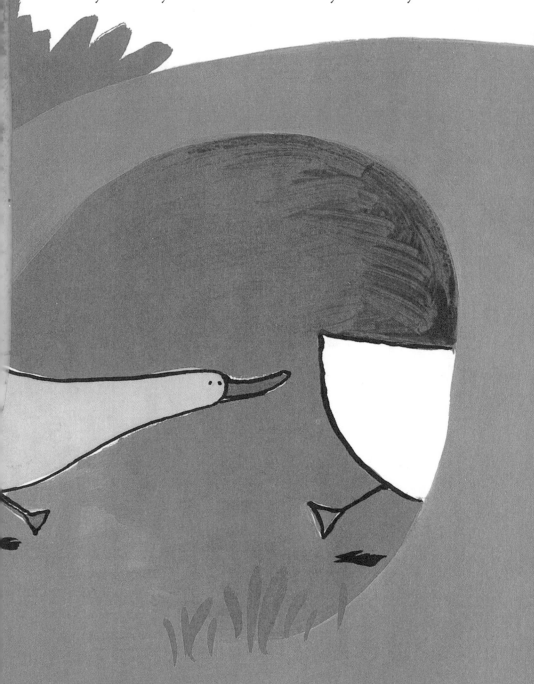

Cocky-Locky went in last.
Henny-Penny heard him cry,
"Run away, Henny-Penny!"

doodle doo!

Henny-Penny started to run.
She ran and ran . . .

. . . and ran!

She ran all the way home.
And she never told the king
the sky was falling!

The Princess
and the
Pea

retold by Harriet Ziefert

illustrated by Emily Bolam

There once was a prince,
who wanted to marry a princess.
But she had to be a *real* princess.

The prince looked and looked.
He met many princesses.

Many, many princesses!
Many, many, many princesses!

But the prince sent
all of them away.
He did not think they
were *real* princesses.

One day there was a big storm.
A princess knocked at the door.

"Come in," said the king.
"Come in," said the queen.

Oh, what a drippy princess!

Her hair was drippy!

Her dress was drippy!

Her shoes were drippy!

But still she said
she was a *real* princess.

The queen said, "I will see.
I will see if this is a *real* princess."
And she went off to make the bed.

First the queen
put a tiny pea
under the mattress.

Next the queen put
1 . . . 2 . . . 3 . . . 4 . . . 5 . . .
6 . . . 7 . . . 8 . . . 9 . . . 10 . . .
mattresses on top of the pea.

Then she put
1 . . . 2 . . . 3 . . . 4 . . . 5 . . .
6 . . . 7 . . . 8 . . . 9 . . . 10 . . . more
mattresses on top of them.

On top of the twenty mattresses,
the queen put twenty down covers.

Then she called the princess.
"Your bed is ready!" she said.

The princess went to bed.

Oh, what a sleepy princess!

In the morning the queen asked,
"How did you sleep?"

And the king asked,
"How did you sleep?"

And the prince asked,
"How did you sleep?"

"I did not sleep,"
said the princess.
"I did not sleep at all!
I did not sleep because there
was a big lump in my bed."

The queen smiled.
The king smiled.

"You must be a *real*
princess!" they said.

"Only a *real* princess could
feel a pea under twenty
mattresses!"

The prince married the princess, because he knew she was a *real* princess!

And the pea?
They saved it for ever and ever.

The Magic Porridge Pot

retold by Harriet Ziefert

illustrated by Emily Bolam

There once was a little girl
who lived with her mother.
They were poor and had
no money for food.

One day, the mother said,
"All I have for you
   is one small cracker.
   Make it last."

The little girl went out to play.
Along came an old man.
"Can you give me something to eat?"
he asked.

"Yes," said the little girl.
She gave him her cracker.

"Thank you," said the old man.
"And here is a present for you."

"This is a magic pot.
When you want to eat, say,
'Little pot, cook!'
When you have eaten all you want,
say, 'Little pot, stop!'"

The little girl ran home.

She put the pot on the table.
She said, "Little pot, cook!"
The pot began to fill
with porridge.

The little girl ate two bowls
of porridge.
Her mother ate two bowls.
They were full and happy.

Then the little girl said,
"Little pot, stop!"
The pot stopped making porridge.

One day, the little girl
went out to play.
Her mother wanted some porridge.
"I don't need to call my little girl,"
she said. "I know what to do."

She looked at the pot and
said, "Cook, little pot."

Nothing happened.

So she said, "Little pot, cook!"
And the little pot began
to fill with porridge.

The mother ate a bowlful.
While she ate, the pot
was filling itself up again.

"Little pot, no more,"
said the mother.

And the pot went on filling.

Porridge began to run over
the top of the pot.
"Little pot, don't cook!"
said the mother.

Porridge poured out of the pot,
over the table,
and onto the floor.
"Don't cook, little pot!"

"Oh dear, oh my!
What are the right words?
What should I say?"
asked the mother.

Faster and faster came the porridge.
Up the walls . . .
out the door . . .

. . . and down the street!

"No, no, porridge pot!"
the mother said.

But nothing stopped the porridge.

The little girl saw a river of porridge coming toward her.

She guessed what had happened.

She shouted, "Little pot, stop!"

The pot heard her and stopped.

Everyone brought spoons.
They ate and ate
until they got back home.

The Little Red Hen

retold by Harriet Ziefert

illustrated by Emily Bolam

A little red hen
lived on a farm with

a dog,

a goose,

and a cat.

One day the little red hen
found some grains of wheat.

"Who will help me plant the wheat?"
asked the little red hen.

"Not I!" said the dog.
"Not I!" said the goose.
"Not I!" said the cat.

"Then I will plant it myself,"
said the little red hen.

And she did!

The little red hen watered
and weeded and watched.
She watched the wheat grow.

One day the wheat was ready to be cut.
"Who will help me cut the wheat?"
asked the little red hen.

"Not I!" said the dog.
"Not I!" said the goose.
"Not I!" said the cat.

"Then I will cut it myself,"
said the little red hen.

And she did!

"Who will help me beat the wheat?"
asked the little red hen.

"Not I!" said the dog.
"Not I!" said the goose.
"Not I!" said the cat.

"Then I will beat it myself,"
said the little red hen.

And she did!

"Who will help me take
the wheat to the mill?"
asked the little red hen.

"Not I!" said the dog.
"Not I!" said the goose.
"Not I!" said the cat.

"Then I will take it myself,"
said the little red hen.

And she did!

The little red hen
came back with flour.

"Who will help me
bake the bread?"
she asked.

"Not I!" said the dog.
"Not I!" said the goose.
"Not I!" said the cat.

"Then I will bake it myself,"
said the little red hen.

And she did!

The bread came out of the oven.
It smelled good. Very good.

The dog, the cat, and the goose
smelled the bread.
They ran to get some.

The little red hen put
the bread on the table.

"Who will help me eat
this good bread?"
asked the little red hen.

"I will," said the goose.

"I will," said the cat.

"I will," said the dog.

"Oh no, you won't!"
said the little red hen.

And she ate it all up herself.

THE UGLY DUCKLING

retold by Harriet Ziefert

illustrated by Emily Bolam

Once upon a time,
nine ducklings hatched.

Eight were pretty
and fluffy and yellow.

But the ninth duckling
did not look like the others.

"You are not like the rest,"
said his mother.

"Ugly duckling! Ugly duckling!"
said the eight other ducklings.
"Ugly duckling! Ugly duckling!
Go away!"

The ugly duckling stayed away
from his eight brothers and sisters.

Once the mother duck took her ducklings
to visit another duck family
on the other side of the lake.

They teased the ugly duckling.
"You can't be a duck!
You can't be a duck!"

"I am a duck!
I am a duck! I am!"
cried the ugly duckling.

And then he ran away.

The ugly duckling hid in some grass.
Soon it got dark.

The ugly duckling was scared
and lonely.
He went to sleep.

The next morning, the ugly duckling
went to look for food.
"What kind of bird are you?"
asked some wild ducks.

"I am a duck," said the ugly duckling.

"You can't be a duck!
 You can't be a duck!"
 they teased.

The ugly duckling ran away
from the wild ducks.

He ran and ran until he came
to another lake.
"I'll stay here," he said.

The ugly duckling stayed all winter.
It was cold. Very cold.
And windy, too.

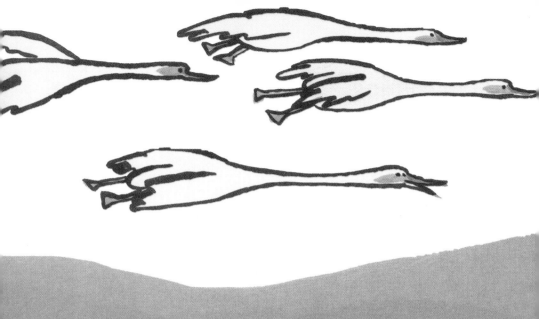

One day, the ugly duckling saw
some swans flying south.
"Come with us!" they called.

"I'm coming," cried the ugly duckling. "Wait for me! Wait for me!"

The ugly duckling flapped his wings.
He tried to take off.
But he couldn't fly very well,
and the swans couldn't wait.

The ugly duckling stayed
by the lake.
He grew . . .

and grew . . .

and grew!

In the spring, the ugly duckling
flapped his wings.
They were big and strong.

"I can fly," he said.
"I can fly!"

He flew to a riverbank.
"Come and stay with us,"
said the swans.

"Who, me?" asked the ugly duckling.
"You don't want me.
  I'm just an ugly duckling."

"A duckling?" they said.

"No, you are a swan.
A beautiful swan, just like us!"